MW00943315

Akea

The Power of Destiny

Book one in the Akea series

Elizabeth Jade

To learn more about this author, please visit:
www.elizabethjade.org

Other books in the *Akea* Series

Book 2: Akea – His Mother's Son

The beautiful illustrations in this book are all by Anthony Wallis.

Pronunciation Guide

Akea	ah-key-uh
Kelleher	kuh-lee-her
Eacnung	ee-ack-nung
Kazakh	kah-zac
Bluinse	blue-in-zee
Leopardo	leo-par-doe
Hortecia	hor-tuh-see-ya
Javier	jay-vee-er
Tinnet	ti-net
Gervazo	ger-var-zoh
Raghnal	rag-nul

All Rights Reserved.
No reproduction, copy or transmission of the publication
may be may be made without written permission. No
paragraph or section of this publication may be
reproduced copied or transmitted save with the written
permission or in accordance with the provisions of the u9

Copyright 2017 Elizabeth Jade
The right of Elizabeth Jade to be identified as the author of
this work has been asserted in accordance with the
Copyright Designs and Patents Act 1988
A copy of this book is deposited with the British Library
London.

ISBN: 978-0-9955729-8-0

Third Edition: 2020

Published by

i2i
PUBLISHING

i2i Publishing. Manchester.
www.i2ipublishing.co.uk

CHAPTER 1

The sun rose slowly over the tree tops, its amber light doing its best to soak up all the dew. Below the darkness of the forest, a wooden lodge stood alone in the shadow of the mountains and rocky outcrops with miles of unspoilt landscape stretched before it. On either side of the lodge there were some large sheds, one of which appeared to be making tiny squeaking sounds.

Inside, on a pile of rugs and scraggy blankets, a beautiful black and white husky was contentedly licking her new born pups while her handsome brown and white mate looked on. She laid her head on the edge of the blanket and closed her eyes as the pups began to feed. Her mate Kelleher, smiled as Eacnung lived up to her name. Kelleher watched his offspring too. It was his responsibility to name the six pups and he had thought long and hard.

"The three males will be Koda, Oston and Darius," he whispered quietly to himself. "And the females will be Madg, Faith and..."

he paused, unable to think of a name that felt right for the last female.

Although her eyes were not open and she was unable to hear, Kelleher knew that she was different from the other pups. She felt special, even though he didn't know why. He left the shed through the dog flap and sat outside gazing about him at the lush grass that would one day be buried under a thick blanket of snow. Then it came to him; she would be called 'Akea'. Feeling extremely proud of himself he set off past the lodge and into another shed where the rest of the huskies lived, and they gathered round him eager to hear his news.

In the early evening, the owner came to inspect the pups, and Eacnung looked up as he came through the door with Kelleher close behind him. "Good girl," he said softly as he sat down beside her and stroked her ears. Eacnung trusted him completely and did not make a sound as he picked up each of her babies in turn. The pups, however, amply made up for her silence as they squeaked and squealed in his large hands. He inspected each one for signs of ill health or defect before replacing them gently back onto the teat they had been so reluctant to leave. Kelleher nudged his leg as he got up.

"Yes boy, you're very clever too," he said with a smile. "Now, you take good care of your pups," he added, and he poured out two bowlfuls of food before heading back to the lodge.

The pups grew rapidly, and it didn't seem long before they were allowed to venture outside. Kelleher led the way out through the dog flap, closely followed by his pups and with Eacnung bringing up the rear. Darius was a little nervous at first, but then he saw Madg rolling around in the grass with Faith and Koda creeping up on her, and it was too good an opportunity to miss. He dived in, closely followed by Oston who then ran around barking in delight. Faith broke away from the game and raced over to Akea who was sitting quietly on a sunny log. However, Akea saw her coming and bounced out of the way leaving Faith to fly over the top and land in a heap on the other side. Akea laughed and nuzzled her sister before returning to her post, and there she sat gazing out into the distance with Faith lying down beside her.

The owner watched them for a while from the lodge door as Kelleher and Eacnung stood guard over their offspring. Then, at the forest edge, a silvery shape appeared from behind a grassy mound. Eacnung howled, and her pups obediently ran to her; all except for Akea who was rooted to the spot; curious but unafraid. She was intrigued by the appearance of a creature she had not seen before; almost mesmerized in fact.

"Akea!" bellowed her father, "Obey your mother at once. Never trifle with a volk, never!" Akea blinked, unable to break free from the wolf's hypnotic stare. Kelleher barked in an attempt to gain his daughter's attention, but it was the appearance of the owner with his twelve bore that caused the wolf to run, breaking his hold on Akea. It was then that she felt her father's paw strike the side of her shoulder. "Get inside now Akea," he growled angrily. "And never disobey me again. A volk spells trouble; always remember that."

The pups were herded back into the shed where their mother comforted them with a small feed and from that point on the owner, Kelleher and Eacnung were extra vigilant whenever the pups were allowed outside. Akea would always scan the edge of the woods in case the wolf came back, but she dare not let her father see her. Every night the wolf plagued her dreams, and although she had no idea what it meant, she was not afraid. Kelleher however, was troubled. The wolf brought back unpleasant memories, for among other things Kelleher knew that he was not a true husky – there was wolf blood in his veins.

One night Akea woke up, went to the dog flap and poked her head out to look round. There stood the wolf, looking at her intently from his grassy mound. He raised his head and howled softly before leaving. Akea desperately wanted to howl back, but she knew that her mother and father would not approve. It seemed as if the wolf was trying to contact her; as if he knew something about her that she was only beginning to learn.

Something stirred deep within her, and she no longer felt that she belonged here with the other huskies.

CHAPTER 2

Many months passed; Akea's siblings had been sold on, and she had begun to feel more and more alone. Now only Faith and Akea remained, chosen by the owner to add to the sled team. They had begun with an individual puppy harness, pulling a piece of snowmobile track or a small log and moved on to being paired for short distances with one of the older more experienced dogs. As well as building up their fitness levels it gave the owner the opportunity to determine the most appropriate place in the sled team for each young dog. It had been so long since she had seen the lone wolf, and her training had been so intense that her thoughts were far less dominated by him, and her father had made her promise that she would tell him at once if the wolf ever came back. She would not disobey her father again, so she tried not to look at the trees too often in case she would be caught and punished. One quiet afternoon, however, while the owner was out, she slipped away from the others and sat staring out at the forest now covered in snow, wondering what had become of the wolf. With a heavy sigh, she joined her family in the shed and lay down sleepily by the dog flap. Suddenly in the distance a howl broke the silence, and Akea put her head out of the flap and stared about her. There was the wolf, running towards her home. She went back inside and reluctantly nudged her sleeping parents.

"Father, the volk is heading this way," she said, hoping that he wouldn't hear her, but Kelleher rose swiftly and dashed out whilst Eacnung, Faith and Akea peered nervously through the flap. Kelleher stopped only a few metres away from the wolf who stood there snarling with his ears flattened and his hackles raised.

Akea looked at her father who snarled back and took the same stance. Things did not look good. As her father lunged forward, the wolf jumped back before lunging at Kelleher's throat. Kelleher twisted and grabbed the wolf by his front leg, but as it went down it lashed out at Kelleher's chest. It was the first fight Akea had ever seen, and it looked like a serious one. Akea went to jump out through the flap to help her father, but Eacnung blocked her way.

"Stop!" she ordered. "We are not strong enough. Besides, protecting the family is your father's role."

As the three dogs watched, the fight became even more intense. Faith buried her face in her mother's coat in fear, and Eacnung turned to comfort her. Then without warning, Akea bounded out of the flap and bit down hard on the wolf's rump. Startled, the wolf released Kelleher and turned to stare at her.

"Well, well, little volk!" he said wryly.

"Why did you call me that?" she asked in a puzzled tone.

"We are distantly related," he replied, looking deep into her eyes.

She stared back and again began to feel the sensation of not belonging here, but before she could say anymore there was a loud howling and the other pack males came rushing towards them. The wolf winked at Akea before running back to the safety of the forest with a string of huskies after him.

Akea ran to her father who lay unconscious and bleeding. The pack gathered round and began licking him anxiously. Just then, a vehicle pulled up next to them and the owner got out, his eyes wide and his mouth open in shock. He gently lifted the husky into the back of his truck, covered him with blankets to keep him warm and drove off. Akea sniffed at her father's blood in the snow before staring out towards the forest. She didn't understand what had happened. Why had this wolf attacked her father and not her? What was he doing here at all?

That night Akea couldn't sleep, so she lay there with the day's events playing over and over in her mind. If only she could make sense of it all. She understood one thing though - the moment the wolf looked into her eyes, she had felt something awaken deep inside that had only stirred before; she felt like a wolf. Not quite knowing why, she quietly left the shed and ran towards the forest. It was gloomy and dark, but

Akea pressed on until she reached a clearing. Stopping in the middle, she raised her head up at the full moon and howled; a long wolf like howl. Almost immediately her call was answered, from right behind her. She turned quickly and there stood the lone wolf.

"Looking for me young volk?" he said.

"Who are you?" she demanded.

"I am Kazakh, the nomad. You were very brave to come to me young volk, but I knew that you would someday."

"My name is Akea!" she grumbled. "How did you know that I would come here?"

"My dear Akea; I know most things," he sniggered as he took a step towards her. Akea began to feel a little uncomfortable. Perhaps it had not been a good idea to come after all.

"I must go back before I'm missed," she said nervously.

"You must stay my young Eacnung," he said as he stepped in front of her. "It is time for you to find your inner wolf. I will teach you."

"Eacnung!" she spluttered - that was her mother's name, and it meant 'bearer of children'.

"You are too forward for your own good, Kazakh. Besides, I cannot go anywhere while my father is injured and you are to blame for that."

Even though this wolf had attacked her father, a large part of her wanted to stay. She wanted to ask him why he had done it, but somehow, she felt that now was not the time; she was so confused.

"I am going back," she said firmly. "But when I am ready, I will call to you Kazakh." And with that she turned and headed home, leaving Kazakh alone in the forest. As she made her way home, she thought about what he had called her - Eacnung. Was he, in his own way, admitting his affection for her or was there more to it than that? She couldn't believe that she was prepared to leave her family to find out. She paused outside the shed, hoping that she hadn't been missed. Her mother would be furious if she found out where she had been, and she wasn't sure if her beloved sister would be able to keep such a great secret. Then there was her father; had he survived the wolf attack? There was only one way to find out, so with a deep breath she crept back into the shed.

CHAPTER 3

Kelleher eventually came home, but it was several months before he was well enough to go back to work. Eacnung fell pregnant again, leaving Faith and Akea to take her place at the sled. No-one spoke about the wolf attack although Akea thought about Kazakh every day. She was growing restless, her inner wolf yearning for the freedom of the forest. She knew that it would soon be time to join Kazakh even though she was still uncertain what lay in store for her, and why he had called her 'Eacnung'. She was annoyed by his secretiveness, yet there was a wildness and slyness about him that she liked.

One morning the owner harnessed her up to the sled without the other dogs. Then he removed a camera from his pocket and took several photographs before sending her back to the others.

"Oh dear!" sighed Eacnung. "It seems as if Faith will be the only one staying." Akea knew all too well what her mother had meant. She was going to be sold, and if that happened then she would never be able to go with Kazakh. That evening she sat alone outside, staring miserably into the distance.

"Are you alright?" asked Faith, sitting down beside her.

"No, not really," sighed Akea.

"It wouldn't have anything to do with your volk friend would it?"

"How did you know about Kazakh?" she asked in surprise.

"I've seen you sneaking off at night to visit him, looking more like a volk with every passing day, and I've heard him calling to you."

"I don't know why I want to join him; I just know that I must. If I am sold I will never get the chance, but if I run away, mother and father will be so upset, and what about you my dearest of sisters?"

Faith could feel how distressed she was, and she began to nuzzle her soothingly, saying softly; "I will be fine; mother will have new pups to distract her soon, and father will continue to be King of the sled." She paused for a moment before adding, "You will start a brand-new life with Kazakh, or wherever your destiny leads you, and I will explain to mother and father as best I can."

"What are you saying? What do you mean?" asked Akea, looking at her sister with a puzzled expression.

"I believe that something great will happen to you, and that one day you will make us all proud, Akea."

Those words touched Akea deeply. She was particularly fond of her sister and would miss her dearly. She licked her affectionately, and then with a mighty bound she raced off into the distance, vanishing into the forest. "Good luck my darling, Akea," Faith whispered softly. "Never will I forget you."

As Akea ran, she thought about what Faith had said. It seemed as if, like Kazakh, she too sensed something different about her. Akea ran deeper into the forest, her leaps and bounds filled with determination and power. Though her eyes brimmed with tears, she fought them back for she had committed herself to this path, and there was no turning back now. She stopped and howled for Kazakh, but there was no answer. She howled again and again, but still Kazakh did not come for her.

"Where are you?" she called desperately, but as she listened for his call she heard instead a chuckling from behind a nearby thicket. "Who's there? Kazakh, is that you?" Then to her horror she found herself face to face with a bear. "Who are you?" she stuttered nervously.

"What does my name matter?" growled the bear, delighted at finding such a young husky all alone.

"Go away!"

"Now that's hardly polite."

"Leave me be, or I'll call Kazakh," she yelled, praying that Kazakh would hear her.

The bear drew closer and closer and Akea began to back away, but soon found she had nowhere to go. "Get away!" she screamed, snapping desperately at the bear and trying to look big, fierce and considerably braver than she felt. This was the biggest of enemies, and on her own she was done for.

"Say goodbye," grinned the bear as he reared up onto his hind legs, and opening his jaws as wide as possible.

Akea closed her eyes tight, wishing that she had stayed to be sold to a new owner. At least she would have been alive instead of about to die. Suddenly a mighty howl rang through the forest and almost like an echo came a second howl. Akea opened her eyes to see two wolves leaping over a fallen tree and into the bear's path. One of them was Kazakh, and the other was a beautiful snowy female. As the ferocious pair snarled and snapped, the bear wisely turned and fled. Unable to maintain her composure, Akea collapsed in a flood of tears and Kazakh rushed over to her and raised her to her feet.

"Now, that's enough of that, Akea. You can't go to pieces every time something goes wrong. The mark of a true volk is to be brave, bold and wise," he said.

"That's right! We must maintain our dignity," said his female companion who had wandered slowly over to them. "Allow me to introduce myself; I am Bluinse."

Recovering herself quickly, Akea rubbed her muzzle against Bluinse in a submissive wolf greeting. "I will be forever grateful, Bluinse." And turning to Kazakh she added, "I thought you were a nomad?"

"I am, but it's always wise to maintain contact with one's family. You can never tell when you might need each other. Come young volk, I will take you to meet my family. I have told them all about you."

As Kazakh led the way, Akea and Bluinse followed along, calmly chatting to one another. Akea wondered just how much Kazakh had told Bluinse.

"Bluinse, did Kazakh tell you that he attacked my father, nearly killing him?" she asked. "I haven't had the nerve to ask him why yet?"

"Kazakh would never make an unprovoked attack on anyone. Are you sure it was him?" she replied, sounding slightly cross.

Feeling confused, Akea walked on in silence, and after a while a large mound came into view. Sitting on top were a small group of higher ranking wolves with the rest of the pack spread beneath them. The alpha female was a glossy black while her mate was a silvery grey, just like Kazakh. Slowly they descended from the mound to greet the trio.

"Welcome Kazakh, our beloved nomad. Pray, who is your husky friend?" said the male wolf, staring at Akea who felt somewhat awkward and lowered her head submissively.

"This father is Akea. Her ancestor was a volk, and she possesses a true volk spirit. I believe she is a volk in all but appearance, and as such belongs with the pack and not with the humans," he stated proudly.

"I am Leopardo," he said to Akea. "If Kazakh says you are a true volk, then you are welcome here."

"And I am Hortercia," smiled the alpha female as she eyed Akea from nose to tail. As she sniffed her face, Akea nudged Hortercia with her nose; her inner wolf coming to the fore. Soon the other pack members came to greet them, but Akea noticed that one young male seemed fearful and kept his distance. Breaking away from the pack she trotted over to him and he flattened himself against the mound and lowered his ears.

"I am Akea," she said smiling, trying to put him at ease.

"I am Javier," he replied nervously.

"I won't hurt you, I promise," she added, nudging him playfully. Relaxing a little, Javier uncoiled himself, and they re-joined the pack together.

Each day after that, Akea woke to the howl of the pack. As the wolf within her began to take over, her voice no longer stood out, but merged beautifully with the others. She and Javier became good friends, and in time she was gradually accepted by the others too. For the moment, everything was perfect.

CHAPTER 4

Early one morning, as Akea was washing herself, she noticed Bluinse and Kazakh slip away from the pack. Kazakh seemed tense, and she wondered if something was wrong. Her curiosity getting the better of her, she stalked after them, determined to find out what was amiss. By keeping out of sight and downwind, she managed to get a good vantage point from which she could both see and hear them, and she was right; things did not look good.

"I hear that you attacked Akea's father," accused Bluinse. "That's not like you at all Kazakh," she sighed.

"She doesn't have to know about her father and what he did all those years ago," he grumbled, turning away from her as he spoke.

"Surely you don't expect her never to ask; after all she did see you attack him." It was clear to Akea that an argument was brewing. "And as for Akea - I had no idea that you wanted to train her up for the position I am to have. What's more, I have a right to it; I am the older female," she snapped.

"You may be older than Akea, but you are not older than me little sister," snarled Kazakh, before continuing in a raised voice. "I admit my feelings for her, and how they have grown, but I must put that aside for now. I know that she is the right one for the task, where as you would abuse your power. You would never be remembered with dignity, honour and love. I know that this is the right path."

"So, you know everything do you? Well my brother, I am sure any feelings she may have for you will vanish when I've told her a few things about you, and I won't give up my goal without a fight either, so you've been warned."

Kazakh finally lost his temper. He leapt up and slashed Bluinse across the head, knocking her to the ground and making Akea gasp.

"You'll pay for this brother," cursed Bluinse as she stood up with a trickle of blood flowing from her cheek. "And so will your beloved Akea," she growled as she turned and left.

Kazakh flopped down with his chin resting on his front paws. He looked more sad than angry now, and Akea's mind was in turmoil over what she had heard. Not sure how he would react, she went over and nuzzled him gently.

"Are you alright?" she asked.

"Yes!" he said, although it sounded more like he was trying to convince himself than Akea. "I suppose you heard everything?"

"I think so. Please tell me about my father; why did you attack him? I have to know," she whispered.

"Very well," agreed Kazakh as he sat up and collected his thoughts. "Many years ago, when my father was a young volk, your father had earned himself quite a reputation. He even went so far as to mate a volk, to be precise the late mother of our present Volk Queen. So, our esteemed volk leader is, in fact, half husky - it has been a heavily guarded secret for many years." Akea seemed truly shocked. She would never have imagined that her father could behave that way, and she felt ashamed.

"Did my mother know about this?"

"Yes, but she never brought it to light. She felt his volk blood was to blame."

"Why do I feel so awful about it?"

"He is your father Akea; you are bound to feel awful about it. You could even be tainted by association if it were common knowledge, as could our Queen."

"What is she like, the Queen I mean?" she asked, curious to know if she resembled her father in any way.

"Perhaps it's time you found out for yourself. Come, I will take you to meet her."

"Oh no, I can't," she cried. "What on earth would I say to her?" Kazakh turned and walked out of the forest without another word. As Akea reluctantly followed him, a thought occurred to her. "Wait a moment! If my father mated her mother, then that makes the Volk Queen my half-sister doesn't it?" Kazakh was reluctant to comment, and Akea felt that there was still more to the story then she had already been told. "Well! Are you going to tell me the rest?

"Not yet!" came the reply.

The scenery around them began to change from forest into mountains. It gave the place a stark, almost forbidding look and had she been alone, Akea felt sure she would have turned back. She asked Kazakh if they could stop for a while, but he pushed on up the mountain regardless. She had no idea what to expect when they reached the Volk Queen. Would she look more like a wolf or a husky? She still didn't quite understand why Kazakh was taking her there at all, but then there always seemed to be so much that she didn't understand. What was the position that Bluinse seemed so determined to have, and had it been wise for Kazakh to cross her so? There were so many questions and Kazakh always seemed to keep the answers to himself. Akea was so distracted that she didn't realise how far they had come. She had never been so high up before, and as they reached a group of rocky outcrops she saw the entrance to a dark cave and a strange sensation came over her. She hung back, but Kazakh took no notice; he stood outside the cave and howled.

"Who's there?" snarled a voice from within the cave and two amber eyes appeared at its entrance.

"It is I great Queen - Kazakh, and I have brought a friend." The shaggy wolf left the cave and sat down, staring at Akea.

"A husky - What is the meaning of this Kazakh?"

"Akea may look like a husky, but within her lies the Great Volk. I have watched her since she was born and I know that she is the perfect choice to succeed you," he said with a smile at Akea's astonished expression. The Queen stared deep into Akea's eyes.

"Perhaps! What do you think of this my half-sister?" So the Queen knew who she was and yet she did not dispute Kazakh's choice of successor.

"Well I don't exactly look the part," queried Akea. "But if you believe that I am the right choice then I do not object to being a leader, as long as you can teach me what I must know." The Wolf Queen smiled and nuzzled her affectionately.

"It is not the outside that matters Akea, but your spirit. A descendent of the Great Volk has a greater claim than any other. Kazakh will train you well and when you are ready you will receive your final lesson from me. Now it is time for you both to go."

She smiled at Akea before heading back into the cave, leaving Kazakh and Akea to return to the pack. They made their way down as silently as they had gone up. She would have liked to ask Kazakh so many things, but she had come to realise that there was little point. He would tell her what she needed to know when he was ready and not before. She would just have to trust him, and her inner wolf; neither had let her down yet, but as they reached the edge of the forest they were shocked to find the wolf pack blocking their path, angry and snarling.

CHAPTER 5

Akea stared in disbelief. She thought that she had been accepted by the pack, so why after all this time would they suddenly turn on her. Equally puzzled Kazakh stepped forward and demanded an explanation.

"You are in no position to demand anything," bellowed his father as the pack opened to let him through. "You have disregarded everything you have ever been taught, and now that I know the truth I intend to put a stop to it." Akea had never seen Leopardo look this angry. "How could you possibly train up this creature in place of your sister?"

"But the Volk Queen has given her approval," argued Kazakh.

"Nonsense! She would never permit such a thing. Accepting your friend into our pack was obviously a mistake; she has turned your head. How could you even consider fathering her pups? You are an alpha, a future pack leader and..." Leopardo paused for a moment, exasperated. "Do our laws mean nothing to you?" Kazakh began to understand what was going on.

"This is your doing, Bluinse," he growled, turning to face his sister whose face bore more of a smile than a snarl, but he couldn't think of anything else to say. To an extent, what Bluinse had told them was true; he did plan to train Akea for a role that would have gone to his sister, but for the right reasons. As for fathering Akea's pups, well he couldn't deny that the thought had crossed his mind. He realised now that he should not have struck Bluinse. Akea stared at Kazakh, wondering why he had fallen silent.

"As for you Akea, you are no longer permitted to remain with the pack," declared his father. "You are banished - forever!"

"No!" snapped Kazakh. "You can't do that; she would never survive alone."

Before he could say anymore, two of the wolves lashed out at Akea. Kazakh tried his best to stop them, but he was roughly pinned to the ground by his father and Akea turned and ran for her life. As the pack chased after her, Kazakh noticed that only

Javier remained, and he could see that he had been severely disciplined. Poor Javier; his only crime had been one of defending Akea's name.

As Akea fled the forest, the only wolf still in pursuit was Bluinse. Suddenly Akea turned and snapped, causing Bluinse to recoil in surprise. Akea seized her chance and raced away, vanishing from view as the snow began to fall thicker and faster. Poor Akea; she was used to being tucked up in her shed or huddled up with Javier or Kazakh for warmth, but now she was on her own and nursing wounds inflicted by the wolves before she fled. She had no idea how far she had run, and she was beginning to feel the strain now. She was cold, tired and hungry. She didn't know where she was or where to look for shelter from the snowstorm. Her pace slowed, and in the end Akea found that she couldn't take another step. She tried her utmost, but to no avail. Finally, she was overcome by exhaustion and collapsed in the snow with the wind howling around her. 'How could it have come to this?' she thought as she closed her eyes, utterly defeated. It was then she felt a cold nose sniffing her coat. She feebly opened her eyes and looked up into the face of a female St Bernard.

"Who are you? What are you doing here?" whimpered Akea.

"I am Idna; it means 'active one' you know; I am sure you will agree there could be no better name for a mountain rescue dog, although I usually rescue people, not dogs." Idna helped Akea to her feet, catching her slightly with the barrel hanging beneath her throat. "Sorry my dear. That's brandy for the humans; they're not as hardy as us. Come! Let me take you somewhere you can get warm."

They set off quite slowly, and after a while they arrived at a large building, with a number of pens outside. Akea looked warily at them, wondering if she was pleased to be rescued after all. When Idna saw her anxious expression she tried to reassure her. "Don't worry; this is an animal shelter where lost and stray animals come to be cared for. Most of them are claimed or rehomed," she said cheerfully, hoping that Akea wouldn't ask about the others, but she did.

"Most of them? What about the rest?"

"The really sick or aggressive are put to sleep, but it is a last resort," she sighed, shaking the snow off her coat. "I can't take care of you my dear, but Adam can." As she spoke, Adam came out with a slip lead in his hand. He approached Akea slowly and dropped the lead over her head.

"Well done girl," he said to Idna, stroking her head as he spoke. Akea gave little resistance as she was led through to an indoor pen. Once inside, Adam locked the door and left her gazing at her new surroundings, feeling just a little claustrophobic. However, the accommodation did have its good points. In the corner, there was a water bowl and, joy of joys, a food bowl full to the brim. The food was not there long for Akea ate hungrily, then after a small drink she settled down for the night; tired, but safe.

The next morning Akea woke to the sound of her kennel door being unlocked and Adam came in with fresh food and water. While she was eating, he sat down beside her and took a brush from his pocket. Slowly and gently he brushed her coat, teasing out all the knots and smearing a little ointment on her healing wounds.

"You're a gentle soul," he smiled as he got up. "I'm sure we will find a new home for you quite soon." With that he left the pen and locked the door behind him. After several days passed in a similar way, Akea noticed a faint whining noise coming from the previously empty kennel next to her. The lower half of the wall between them was made of brick so that rescued dogs would not distress one another, but the top half was made of mesh. Akea went over to the wall and stood on her hind legs, resting her front paws against the bottom of the mesh. She gasped in horror at the state of the dog on the other side.

The poor thing had hardly any fur and was wearing a thick dog jacket to keep it warm. It bore the wounds and scars of ill treatment and was thinner than any creature she had ever seen. She called softly to it, hoping to be of some comfort.

The dog's ears pricked up at the sound of her voice, and as it turned its head to look at her, Akea cried out in disbelief: "Faith!"

CHAPTER 6

Akea couldn't believe her own eyes. How could her dear sister have become this wretched creature? When she had left home that fateful night, Faith had assured her that all would be well, yet things had obviously gone wrong, terribly wrong indeed.

"Oh Faith, my dearest sister," she cried, almost in tears. "I nearly didn't recognise you. What on earth has happened?" Faith yawned feebly before she answered in a voice so weak that Akea was barely able to hear her.

"I was sold just after you went away, and my new master was such a horrid man. All his dogs were skinny, snappy and abused. He made us work so hard, and for so little food, and if we fought over what little food there was or made any mistakes when working, then he beat us with a huge stick. He made me work in a full sled team before I could manage it. It was so awful!" she explained. "In the end the authorities found out and took us all away." Akea began to feel guilty. She had left that night to avoid being sold and sent away from Kazakh. If only she had stayed, none of this would have happened.

"Oh Faith! This is all my fault," she whimpered. "If I had allowed myself to be sold..."

"No Akea," interrupted her sister. "Our owner had fallen on hard times, and I was not the only dog to be sold. It would have changed nothing if you had stayed."

Akea felt devastated by her sister's tragic story. She had never imagined that humans could be so cruel and heartless, but then her so called wolf friends had turned on her too. She would never trust another living soul again - human or wolf.

"It seems we have both been unlucky," sighed Akea. Faith looked puzzled and then she remembered why Akea had left home in the first place.

"Wait a moment," she said, coughing badly before she could continue. "You left to be with Kazakh. How could you possibly have come to be in here?"

Akea related her story to Faith who listened sleepily, feeling Akea's heartache in every word.

"I am sorry things have turned out so. I think you would have made a great Volk Queen." The door to Faith's pen was opened, and two men came in. As one of them knelt beside her and opened a small leather case, Faith looked up at Akea and whispered, "And I believe you still will."

Just then, there was a clanking of doors and Akea's pen was opened. Adam slipped on the lead and took her outside to where a man and a woman stood waiting. The friendly couple patted her for a while; saying how beautiful and gentle she was. Then to Akea's surprise, they took her for a walk. She wasn't sure that she liked this much after the freedom of the forest, but she was too distressed by the thought of poor Faith to give it any real consideration. She couldn't help wondering what had befallen the rest of her family, but even Faith would not be able to answer that. She could only pray that her mother and father were alright and that they had forgiven her for running away.

When they returned to the rescue centre, Akea was not put back in her pen, but tethered up outside. While the couple talked with Adam and signed her release papers, two men came out of the kennels carrying an animal on a stretcher, covered with a blanket. As the men turned down the side of the office Akea saw the poor creature's face and a lump came to her throat. It was Faith! Akea was heartbroken, but before she could run to her she was lifted into the back of a Landrover, the door was shut tight, and the vehicle drove away from the kennels and away from Faith.

"Run free my dear Faith," sniffed Akea as the kennels disappeared from view. "I shall miss you, but at least you will not suffer anymore."

She whimpered quietly as they bumped along, hoping that her new owners turned out to be more reliable than Faith's had. It was not the most comfortable ride, and Akea was relieved when the vehicle came to a stop. She could see a cabin and several sheds, one with a strange looking dog lying outside; well at least she wouldn't be lonely here. The man opened the boot, and Akea jumped down, feeling quite relieved that all the bumping about was over. They led her over to the other dog, and she greeted him submissively. Happy that they were getting along alright, her new owners slipped off Akea's lead and headed for the cabin, leaving her with her new friend.

"Greetings, I am Akea. Who are you?" she asked.

"I am Gervaso," he replied.

"Forgive me, but you're not a pure husky are you?"

"You are very observant for one so young Akea, for I am indeed part husky and part volk." Akea wasn't sure whether she had seen or felt the difference in him.

"I have a half-sister who is part volk," she said. "And I have some volk in me too."

"Come," he said with a smile. "It is time to introduce you to the others." And with that he walked away leaving Akea to follow.

The other dogs were equally friendly, and she began to feel quite at home. It felt good to be part of a pack again. She still wondered what had become of the rest of her family, and of Kazakh and Javier, but she would never know.

One particular husky seemed to have his eyes fixed on her almost all the time. He was brown and white like her father, and his name was Raghnal, 'the strong one'. He was a handsome animal with a tendency to strut up and down. The female huskies were evidently besotted with him, and whenever he spoke they just seemed to melt away as if they were hypnotised by him. Akea discovered that he was also the pack leader and the head of the sled team. Try as she might, she couldn't seem to stop herself from blushing slightly when he spoke to her; although she managed to hide it from the others.

"Hey there, beautiful!" he called, raising his eyebrows at Akea and making her blush yet again. As he walked away, Adine came to sit by her. Her name meant 'tenderness' and she certainly spoke with this admirable quality.

"Isn't he handsome?" she swooned.

"He's certainly full of himself," whispered Akea, taking Adine quite by surprise.

The owners thought highly of Raghnal as did all the other dogs, except for Gervaso and herself. It seemed they both thought he was too self-assured. Akea did think that he was a splendid looking animal, but no dog would ever be as handsome as Kazakh. Oh, how she missed him. She felt sure that she would never see him again, although his face would always linger in her mind. Leopardo and Hortercia would never allow such a friendship to exist, and now she would never know if she would have ended up his mate or the next Volk Queen. It was beginning to feel like a distant dream, yet part of her refused to give up. The Volk Queen had given her approval, and her sister's fate had shown her that change can come when you least expect it.

CHAPTER 7

As the months rolled by, Akea became a vital member of the sled team. She was fast, strong and had unbeatable stamina, which was one of the reasons that Raghnal was so taken with her. Akea could not have been less interested in him. She preferred to spend her free time talking with Gervaso. The wolf in him helped her to remember that inside she too was different. The other females still insisted that Raghnal was irresistibly handsome and would often mention this to Akea, but her reply was always the same: "He's such a flirt," she would grumble. The others would laugh, thinking the whole thing a joke, but Akea meant every word.

Akea enjoyed the sense of achievement she gained from pulling a sled, and was always excited when their owner, John prepared to go down to the village. One morning she watched him getting the sled out and checking its condition before harnessing up his team. Raghnal came over to her with his tail swishing to and fro. As he passed by, he brushed her face with his tail and Akea grumbled under her breath; irritated by his persistent flirting. Once he was sure that all was in order, John selected his team.

"Milo! Sweep!" he called, and two black and white huskies raced forward. They were the wheel dogs, the ones harnessed up directly in front of the sled. Then he called for Akea and Shani. They were the swing dogs, the ones with the strength to help swing the team along the turns and curves of the trail. Finally, he selected Raghnal and Swift as his lead dogs; they would set the pace and find the trail. If he had been expecting to pull a heavy load then he would have selected additional team dogs to pull between the swing and wheel dogs, so Akea knew this was to be a light load, most probably from the store.

Once everything was checked and re-checked, John climbed on and gathered up his reigns. "Hike, hike," he yelled and the dogs set off on the long journey down to the village, gathering speed quite quickly with their empty sled. They raced along the track past the thinning trees with the dogs panting vigorously. It was hard work, but Akea loved it. At long last they stopped outside the village store and John tethered his team to a post before going inside, leaving his dogs to lie down and snooze until his return.

About an hour later John came out with his supplies and loaded them onto the sled, securing them firmly before untethering his dogs and setting off back up the hillside. The return journey was always harder than the decent, but the load was not too heavy and the six dogs were more than adequate for the task. They arrived back in good spirits, and as John removed his dogs from their harnesses, they set about playing happily together.

The next day, as Akea was lying down outside with her breath steaming out over the snow-covered ground, she heard John's wife Rachael calling her name. She ran obediently to her mistress who slipped a lead over her head and led her round to the side of the cabin towards a small chain-fenced enclosure. After she was released inside her mistress turned away, and Akea lay down, wondering why she had been put in here. It wasn't long before the door opened again, and Raghnal entered the enclosure.

"Hey gorgeous!" he called in a charming voice. "You look stunning today." Akea stood up defensively and demanded an explanation for their confinement. "Don't you know?" he asked in a curious tone that made her uneasy, but then he saw Akea shaking her head and realised that she honestly had no idea at all. "Why, you and I are here to mate," he explained. Akea sat down suddenly; she hadn't expected that at all. "Don't look so surprised; you're the best dog on the team next to me. Just think of the pups we could raise." Raghnal was quite surprised by Akea's shocked response, but remained convinced that she could be persuaded.

"No Raghnal, don't even think about it," said Akea firmly, but Raghnal became angry and as he circled her, he began to growl.

"If you think I'm leaving here without doing my duty then you are quite mistaken,

Akea. I have a reputation to uphold, and you would be unwise to cross me."

"And if you think you can threaten me into submission then you are the one who is mistaken Raghnal," she snarled as she jumped to her feet, flattening her ears in an aggressive posture.

Poor Raghnal was furious, and he was not about to have his reputation ruined by this young upstart. As he drew nearer, Akea took a deep breath, searching for the inner wolf that had been hidden for so long, but as she opened her mouth it was not her own voice that rang out, but a much deeper, richer one.

"Raghnal! Step away from my mate!" Akea looked round in astonishment.

"Kazakh!" she cried both happy and relieved to see him alive and well. The mighty wolf stood with his ears flat and his hackles raised, front paws on the mesh fence, growling ferociously.

"Excuse me volk, but in case you hadn't noticed this lovely lady is a husky, not a volk, and she has been selected as my mate," snapped Raghnal. Akea looked at Kazakh with a mixture of joy and curiosity.

"How do you know his name Kazakh?"

"The final part of our discussion regarding your half-sister," began Kazakh, noting her puzzled expression with a barely concealed grin. "Before she became Queen, your half-sister met a husky, a skinny and frightened creature that she cared for until he was strong and bold, but he abused her kindness and affection by assaulting one of her pack members and disappearing virtually without trace. By the time they had tracked him down; he was the proud father of a very young litter of husky pups."

"Oh how awful," cried Akea. "She must have been so upset, but who would do such a thing?"

"He's right behind you, aren't you Raghnal?" Akea stared a Raghnal, her mouth open in astonishment. There had always been something about him that she didn't like, but she would never have believed it would be something like this.

"How dare you!" she growled, feeling the anger deep inside of her. "How dare you," she screamed, and with that she struck

Raghnal with a force so strong that he was knocked to the ground and winded.

"That's my girl," smiled Kazakh as he turned to leave, knowing instinctively that Akea would follow, and with a parting snarl at Raghnal, she cleared the low-level fence with ease. As they raced away Akea recalled how this was the second time she had left her home to be with Kazakh, and as things had gone badly wrong the first time, she desperately hoped that history would not repeat itself.

"Did you mean it when you said that I was your mate?" she asked as she slowed to a walking pace. "What about your father and the laws he spoke of?" Kazakh gave her a brief sideways glance and slowed to match her pace before answering.

"I have severed all ties with my pack, so no-one can stop me. I don't blame my father for what happened; he has been following ancient laws his entire life, but that does not necessarily mean they are right. I know this is the right course, and I hope that one day my father will understand. We will start a new pack if you will have me."

"I have spent my whole life waiting to be with you Kazakh and I will be proud to be your mate," she smiled. As Akea looked at Kazakh she knew there were no words to express the joy that she felt at that moment, but there was one thing that still troubled her. "What about Bluinse and the role of Volk Queen?" she enquired.

"The Volk Queen knows that you are the one destined to succeed her. All that matters now is that you reach her in time."

CHAPTER 8

Kazakh and Akea had been running for several days, pausing only briefly to rest or feed. By night fall they barely had the energy to find a suitable place to curl up together and snatch a few hours of decent sleep. They didn't relax their pace until the tall rocky mountains of the Wolf Queen's den came into view, with the dense forest of Kazakh's former residence spread menacingly beneath it.

"Are you sure we shouldn't try and speak with your father one last time?" asked Akea. "I would not wish there to be any hate between us if it could be helped." But Kazakh assured her that it was too great a risk.

"If they saw us together, they would kill us both. They're mad enough as it is because of Bluinse, so there's no way I'm going anywhere near them right now." Those words made Akea restless; she wanted to ask him what had happened, but the mention of his sister reminded her that she had lost her own dear sister since they had last met.

Akea sighed deeply as she told him of her loss and he in turn nuzzled and licked her. Then, as it grew dark, they spent an affectionate night together beneath a starry sky.

They set off again at first light, full of determination and hope, but as they walked along, Akea began to think about what Kazakh had said regarding his sister.

"What happened with Bluinse?" she asked gently, hoping that his usual reserve would not move him to side-step the answer. Kazakh seemed troubled by her question, but they were a pair now, and he must tell her.

"When she heard that I was leaving for good, she just disappeared. She must have known I would come looking for you, yet I haven't seen her, and now I'm worried that she's going to do something dreadful."

They walked on in silence, neither daring to put their worst fears into words until they reached the base of the mountains. It was then that a strange sensation came over Akea, and without warning she bolted up the mountainside towards the Wolf Queen's home.

"Hey!" called Kazakh. "What's going on?" But this time it was Akea's turn to race off without an answer, and there was nothing he could do. He chased after her, and as he caught up he repeated his question.

"Something's wrong," she answered, stopping for a moment and turning to him with a look in her eyes that Kazakh had never seen before; a detached, faraway look that was almost eerie. "I have to get up there before it's too late." Without waiting for his response, Akea raced on up the mountainside with determination in every stride and all Kazakh could do was try and keep up.

The Wolf Queen lay peacefully outside her cave, soaking up the afternoon sun and waiting for Kazakh to keep his word. Her heart was not as strong as it was and she knew that her time was not far off, but where was Akea? Kazakh had promised to bring her even if it cost him his life. A noise below drew her to the edge of the outcrop, but she already knew that it was not Akea approaching. As she suspected, it was Bluinse who was marching slowly up the mountain towards her. She needed Akea here now, and there was only one thing left that she could do. She returned to the cave entrance and lay down again; closing her eyes she reached out to Akea with all the strength she could muster.

Meanwhile, Akea and Kazakh had paused for just a moment to catch their breath when suddenly a gunshot ripped through the air, and Kazakh fell to the ground, a huge wound in his side. Horrified, Akea looked up and saw a man with a bushy red beard reloading his gun. Something inside her snapped, and with a mighty wolf howl she leaped on him before he could even think about raising his gun again. As he fell he struck his arm heavily against a rock, losing his grip on the gun which tumbled down the mountain leaving him defenceless. Akea returned to Kazakh and stood over him protectively while the man staggered to his feet, clutching his injured arm and wondering why he was not fighting for his life. He took one brief look at Akea's snarling face and fled. Akea could sense the Wolf Queen's desperation, but her mate lay seriously wounded, and she felt torn between love and duty.

"Go!" ordered Kazakh. "You are the chosen descendent of the Great Volk, and you must take your place as Queen, and you must do it for me because I love you."

Akea's eyes stung with tears. She desperately wanted to stay, but she knew that Kazakh was right. Just then she saw a small one-dog sled heading in her direction and realised that the gun shot had alerted the forest rangers. She waited for them to notice Kazakh before running away, praying that they would help him. She thought the husky with the ranger looked rather like Raghnal, but that wasn't possible. She decided to risk a shortcut in an attempt to reach the Wolf Queen first, but the ground was far more treacherous this way and she slipped badly, scrabbling at the edge of an outcrop. Her eyes blurred as she caught sight of the rugged landscape beneath her, but with a snarl of determination she scrambled back up; she simply had to get there before it was too late.

CHAPTER 9

A lone white wolf stood on the edge of a rocky outcrop, surveying the scene before her with a feeling of triumph. Akea was nowhere in sight, and the old Queen lay alone and defenceless outside her den.

"Time's up your majesty," she said confidently. "I am here to claim what is mine by right." The Queen stood up slowly and looking into the wolf's eyes sighed deeply before she spoke.

"What is the meaning of this Bluinse? You know that my half-sister Akea has been chosen to take my place. You forfeited the right to it long ago, and I will not give you my blessing now." Bluinse glared back, unconcerned.

"Akea cannot help you now; she has left with Kazakh and they will not risk being found together anywhere near here. I will take your place, with or without your blessing, and there is nothing you can do." With that Bluinse leaped forwards and knocked the Queen to the ground, but as she fell the mountain resounded to a harrowing wolf cry. Bluinse turned, expecting to see an entire wolf pack behind her and was astonished to find that there was only one, solitary creature.

"Bluinse, step away from the Queen," demanded Akea, her eyes bright and fierce.

"And let you take the Queen-ship? Over my dead body," came the reply.

"So be it!"

Akea and Bluinse snarled and snapped, pacing to and fro before leaping onto each other and fighting ferociously. As a wolf, Bluinse should have had the advantage, after all Kazakh would have killed Akea's father if she had not intervened, yet they appeared to be evenly matched, for Akea was no longer acting like a husky, but like a true wolf. As Akea lunged for her throat, Bluinse stumbled and slipped off the edge of the crag, dragging Akea part of the way down with her. By letting go of Bluinse, Akea managed to stop herself from sliding any further, but her position was far from safe. Bluinse, her eyes wide with fear now instead of anger, was still scrabbling for a foothold, but she could not find one. Akea cried out as

Bluinse fell to her death, but she could do nothing to help her.

Akea looked up to find the Queen's silvery figure peering over the edge in relief. Focusing hard, Akea began to scramble back up, and when she was almost there the Queen reached out and pulled her over the edge and back onto level ground. Overcome by shock and exhaustion Akea collapsed, breathing heavily.

"Thank you, sister," gasped Akea and the Queen smiled.

"Under the circumstances I think you may call me Tinnet," she said affectionately. "You have done well my dear Akea, now come inside the den and rest. Tomorrow is a new day, and there is still much to be done."

Over the week that followed Bluinse's death, Akea received her final training from Tinnet, her half-sister and Queen. Then at long last she received her blessing. As she rested outside the cave, Akea thought of all that she had been through to reach this moment, but with such thoughts came memories of Kazakh and she wondered if his parents were aware of what had befallen both Kazakh and Bluinse. Without a word, Akea stood up and began to walk down the mountain. The old queen smiled; she didn't need to ask where Akea was going for she already knew. Akea made her way through the forest, feeling the cold snow beneath her feet until she reached the fallen tree that marked the edge of their territory and there, just as she had expected, stood Kazakh's former pack.

"Well, well Akea," declared Leopardo. "I never thought to see you again. You are very stupid to have come back here, especially alone."

"I have news, Sir," said Akea in a solemn tone. "Bluinse is dead!" In the stunned silence that followed, Akea was able to explain about both Bluinse and Kazakh. "I am sorry Leopardo, Hortercia, I didn't mean for it to happen this way. I have finished my training and received the Volk Queen's blessing, but I would like so much to have your blessing too as I take my rightful place as Queen over this land."

Leopardo and Hortercia looked at one another and nodded; it was time to forget the past.

"My dear girl," began Hortercia. "We have all misjudged you. Bluinse was always headstrong, and Kazakh always seemed to know more about what was going on than the rest of us. We would be proud to give you our blessing, and to accept you as Queen."

"And me as King!" said a cheery voice from behind them, and they all turned to find Kazakh standing there; a small bald patch on one side. He was limping a little, but he was still strong enough to take Akea's weight as she pushed him down and licked him tenderly.

"I've missed you," cried Akea with tears running down her cheeks. "I didn't know if I would ever see you again."

"Well my love, I have missed you too," he replied. As he stood up they began to lick each other vigorously round the muzzle, showing to all the bond between them, and as the pack joined together in greeting them, Leopardo knew that there was just one thing left to be done.

CHAPTER 10

The following afternoon, all the wolves gathered outside the Wolf Queen's den. There was an air of excitement and anticipation as they greeted one another, then a hush descended as Leopardo made his way forward. Nodding respectfully to the old Queen, he climbed onto the rock by the den entrance and sat down, looking out over his pack.

"Noble volk," he began, "In recent times we have faced all manner of difficulties, through which we have preserved our beliefs, strange though they may seem to others, and defended our unity. However, we have learned that such unity comes in many forms, and this has certainly proved true with Akea. Although a husky by birth, she has put her trust in her volk instincts and in so doing has brought a son and his family back together, despite the disloyalty of Bluinse. As a descendent of the Great Volk and chosen successor of our noble Queen, she will today be crowned Queen of this land in one of our oldest and most treasured traditions."

A chorus of wolf howls and barks filled the air, echoing around the mountain tops like the sound of an earthquake, and fading away as Akea made her way through the pack and sat down beside the Wolf Queen. She looked at Kazakh, who winked at her. This was Akea's big moment, and she wished her family, especially her sister Faith could have been there, but instead of beginning the ceremony as she had expected, she found that Leopardo had a further declaration to make.

"There comes a point in any leader's life when they must stand down in place of their successor, and I have decided that this great day should hold a double celebration," he declared as a faint murmur rippled through the crowd. "Kazakh, my son has proven himself to be an alpha male without equal; brave, knowledgeable and wise, and it gives me considerable pleasure to hand over the leadership of this pack to him....and to his mate, Akea."

The wolves had begun to voice their approval, but as they heard Akea's name mentioned again they fell silent as the full meaning of Leopardo's words were taken in. The Wolf Queen had always been a solitary wolf whose successor was chosen in the final years of her reign, but having married Kazakh, Akea would be uniting these two roles for the first time in the history of the pack. It was into this stunned silence that the Wolf Queen began her own short speech of approval, and as Akea stood for the ceremony she noticed a familiar figure standing proudly at the edge of the pack.

"Father!" she cried in amazement. He may have been rather grey around the muzzle, but there was no mistaking him. Kelleher made his way through to his daughters and bowed low before licking Akea affectionately. Then he turned to Tinnet. It was the first time he had seen his eldest child.

"Am I forgiven for abandoning your mother all those years ago," he whispered so that no-one else would hear.

"Now is the time to look forwards and not back," she answered with a small nod.

"How did you find us?" asked Akea.

"I told him!" came a voice from the shadows. It was Raghnal! "I have known where Tinnet's den was as long as Kazakh has," he smiled. "It seemed only right that a father should witness his daughter's happiest day."

"But how did you know?"

"A day or two after you left I followed you, determined to make amends. When I found out what was going on I knew the best way to do so was to fetch Kelleher. All I ask in return is that you permit me to stay." Akea looked at her half-sister for it was her trust that Raghnal had broken all those years ago. The old Queen nodded her approval and Raghnal sat down among his wolf cousins, setting off the murmuring once more.

Kelleher looked about him and smiled. On the day that Akea was born, he had sensed that she was special, that she was destined for something great, and indeed on this day extraordinary things had been achieved - past errors had been pardoned, a father had been reunited with his children, and huskies and wolves had come together as one. The old Queen barked for silence; the ceremony was about to begin and a new era was about to dawn.

Thank you for reading
Akea – The power of Destiny

If you have enjoyed it, I hope you will tell
your friends or leave a brief review
on Amazon or Goodreads.

Be sure to subscribe to my newsletter or blog
at www.elizabethjade.org and be among the
first to know when a new title is available.

Thanks again for reading
Akea – The Power of Destiny

Best Wishes
Elizabeth Jade